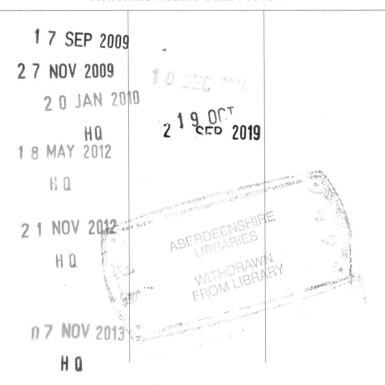
CASSIDY, Anne

Jumping Josie

D1513189

2591633

First published in 2004 by
Franklin Watts
338 Euston Road
London
NW1 3BH

Franklin Watts Australia
Level 17 / 207 Kent Street
Sydney
NSW 2000

A CIP catalogue record for this book is available
from the British Library.

ISBN 978 0 7496 5774 1

Series Editor: Jackie Hamley
Series Advisors: Dr Barrie Wade, Dr Hilary Minns
Design: Peter Scoulding

Printed in China

Franklin Watts is a division of
Hachette Children's Books.

For Josie Morey – A.C.

Jumping Josie

Written by
Anne Cassidy

Illustrated by
Sean Julian

W
FRANKLIN WATTS
LONDON • SYDNEY

Anne Cassidy

"I wrote this story after watching frogs leap about in my garden. I hope you enjoy it!"

Sean Julian

"My favourite animals to paint are bears. Frogs are difficult to paint as they jump away!"

Josie loved
to jump.

5

"Look!" she said.

"I can jump higher and higher!"

One day, Josie
jumped too high.

She landed in the
next garden!

12

"I don't like this garden," said Josie. "There's no pond and no grass!"

13

Josie tried to jump back to
her own garden.

"The fence is too high!"
she said.

She tried to get through
a hole.

The hole is too small!"
she said.

Josie looked around. She
saw just what she needed.

18

It was a trampoline.
Josie jumped and
jumped and
jumped.

She landed back in the pond in her own garden. Home at last!